Beast Hunter

Kathryn White

Für Jonathan-Liebe von der Tante Kath

First published 2011 by A & C Black,
an imprint of Bloomsbury Publishing Plc
50 Bedford Square, London WC1B 3DP

www.acblack.com

ISBN 978-14081-4265-3

A CIP catalogue for this book is available from the British Library.

Printed and bound in Great Britain
by CPI Cox and Wyman, Reading, RG1 8EX

recommended by

www.catchup.org

Catch Up is a not-for-profit charity which
aims to address the problem of
underachievement that has its roots in
literacy and numeracy difficulties.

BEAST HUNTER

Contents

1	Joker	7
2	True Lies	17
3	Evidence	25
4	Blood Trail	32
5	The Battle	43
6	The Catch	52
7	Afterwards	58

Chapter 1

Joker

No one likes to be turned into a joke.

But that happened to me when I saw a crocodile in the old quarry pond near my home.

It was the second week of the holidays. I was already bored and I had another month to go before term started. Then I'd be back to being bored at school again.

Anyway, I was kicking about down at the quarry.

The quarry is very deep, and it's very dangerous because it's full of old machines. There's a sign up saying:

NO SWIMMING

and other signs that say:

DANGER

My mate Ryan once put on his snorkel and went down to have a look.

When he came up I thought he was going to explode, he was so thrilled.

"Amazing!" he gasped.

"What's in there?" I asked.

"Everything's in there!" said Ryan. "There's something big. I think it might be a tractor."

"No way," I said.

I wanted to get into the murky water and see for myself.

"And watch this," said Ryan.

He dived back in and swam a short way,
then stood up on something hidden just below
the surface.

It looked like he was walking on water. In fact, he was standing on the tractor.

"This will make a great diving platform," he said.

It had been the best bit of last year, finding all those old, rusty machines in the quarry.

I told Ryan not to tell anyone else about it. I wanted it to be our secret.

But you can put Ryan's fingers in a mincer, you can poke him with hot irons and he still won't keep his mouth shut.

He told everyone. He might as well have stood on top of that tractor with a microphone.

I was fed up. I wanted to explore the quarry before anyone else did. But Ryan's my mate, so I gave him an ear-bashing, he gave me his latest Call of Duty game, and I forgave him.

Two days after we found it, the place was full of kids.

It was a great summer. We had such a laugh diving from the tractor.

That was until the death.

It was near the end of summer and the quarry was full. There were loads of kids messing around, having fun.

Nobody knew that Adrian Parsons was trapped inside one of the machines.

His mum called the police when he didn't come home. It took the police divers an hour to find him.

I shiver now, when I think I was swimming about, having fun, when someone below me was dying.

No one ever went swimming there again.

But I often went back to watch the newts and to remember those fantastic days before Adrian died.

So there I was, sitting looking into the water, when I saw something.

I saw half a metre of a reptile's tail. It slid silently down from the bank and vanished into the dark reeds.

I stood staring at the reeds and thought about what I'd just seen. Could there really be a croc in there? Awesome!

I mean, I'd only ever seen a croc on TV. It could have been an alligator. But it was one of them.

I wasn't sure who I was going to tell or what I was going to say. I felt excited and scared.

I took off as fast as lightning.

Chapter 2

True Lies

Ryan had gone to his dad in Australia for the summer. I knew there were crocs there. Ryan saw them on the river bank, and he sometimes ate crocodile steak for dinner.

It sounded gross but Ryan said that it was one less croc in the river to worry about.

I sent him an email telling him about the croc. He just said:

```
ha, ha, ha, who's a
joker?
```

It's pretty sad when your best mate doesn't believe you.

But who else would believe me?

I looked up crocs on the internet. They don't just bite – they hold you in their jaws and do a death roll to tear you apart. It's pretty nasty stuff.

I thought I had better tell an adult.

First I told Mum.

Mum shook her head. "You've been watching way too much Jungle Wars," she said.

"Honest, Mum, I saw a croc," I said.

"You are funny," said Mum. "Last year you said you saw a space ship."

"Well, that balloon did look pretty odd," I said.

"A croc in the quarry!" said Mum with a laugh. And that was that.

Mum didn't believe me. I needed to find someone who would believe me.

So I set off to the police station.

* * *

The officer took me into a room and sat me down. He was pretty nice to start with.

"Now what can I do for you?" he asked, smiling at me.

"I saw a crocodile in the quarry," I said.

The officer gave me a very strange look. Then he said, "I see. Tell me more."

"Well," I said, "I was at the quarry yesterday and I saw a big reptile's tail. It was long and brownish-green."

The officer shook his head. Then he said, "Why aren't you in school?"

"Because it's the summer holidays," I said.

"Ah," said the officer. "That explains it."

"What do you mean?" I asked.

"The way I see it," said the officer, "you're bored, and you thought it would be fun to pretend that you had seen a crocodile."

Now he wasn't smiling. "But did you know that it's crime to waste police time?"

I couldn't blame the officer for thinking I was lying. How could a crocodile get into the quarry?

The whole thing was crazy. But I knew what I'd seen.

The officer wasn't going to help. "I must have made a mistake," I said, and I got up to leave.

* * *

As I walked out of the police station I realised that sorting out the crocodile was not going to be easy. I was on my own.

But then I saw a white van parked up. It had PEST CONTROL on the side.

Now, I didn't know what counted as a pest. Wasps? Rats? Stray dogs? Maybe ... but what about a crocodile?

I needed to find out.

Chapter 3

Evidence

The pest control man came out of a house carrying a stun stick and a very angry badger in a cage.

"Don't worry, Mrs Jones," he said to an old lady standing at the door. "I'll let the badger out twenty miles away. You won't see him again."

The pest control man saw me standing by his van but didn't say anything. Like a true hunter, he watched and waited.

He put the badger in the back, then went round to the front cab. He was about to jump in when I stopped him.

"You got a problem?" he said.

"Yes. I need your help," I said.

"Really?" he said, looking hard at me.

"There's a crocodile in the quarry. It's big and it's going to kill someone."

I said it fast, before he could laugh in my face.

But he didn't laugh.

He said, "Go to the police."

"I've been to the police. They think I'm wasting their time," I replied.

He looked at his van keys. I could tell he was thinking about whether he should just drive off, or carry on listening to me.

"Look, I know it's crazy but it's true. I saw a reptile's tail going into the reeds. And this beast is big, I mean, *big*," I said. "Someone's going to get killed."

"Where do you think a croc's come from?" he asked.

"I don't know," I said.

He took a card from his pocket and gave it to me.

"Sometimes people smuggle snakes into the country. The idiots! The police call me in to catch the most deadly snakes. So," he said, "it's possible a smuggler could bring a croc in. But why here?"

"Maybe it's been here for a while? Perhaps it has been living in the countryside and found its way to our quarry?" I said.

"OK," he said. "Tell you what. Bring me a photo to prove you're telling the truth, and I'll help."

He got into his van.

"What's your name?" he said.

"Jacob," I replied.

"Jacob the Beast Hunter, eh? Good luck," he called.

I watched his van speed away. With his help, I could track down this crocodile.

I looked at the card he had given me and laughed.

```
┌─────────────────────────────────┐
│                                  │
│            T.T.T.                │
│     Toby's Trace and Trap        │
│      Best for the pest.          │
│                                  │
└─────────────────────────────────┘
```

Toby was going to help me. All I needed
was a photo.

Chapter 4

Blood Trail

I bought a leg of lamb at the supermarket.
I hadn't planned to spend the money Gran and
Gramps gave me for my birthday on meat.
But sometimes you have to do strange things.

I stuffed the meat into my rucksack along with an old tow rope and my phone.

I kept thinking that the croc might have left the quarry and moved into someone's swimming pool. They did that in films all the time. But I didn't know anyone who had a swimming pool around here.

As I walked down to the quarry, I met an old man on his way out.

"Have you seen a little dog?" he asked me. "Wags has vanished. I've looked everywhere."

"Sorry, I haven't seen a dog," I said.

In my mind I could see a horrible picture of Wags in the jaws of a big croc, doing a death roll.

"He ran off, barking, and the next minute I heard a splash and Wags was gone," said the man.

I didn't want to say what I thought had happened. "If I see him, I'll take him to the police," I said.

The man nodded and walked off. I felt bad. But the guy didn't know how lucky he was; the crocodile could have killed him instead of Wags.

I crept up to the pond and looked down below the surface. It was all very still and silent, but for the gentle buzz of insects.

"I know you're in there," I whispered.

I had a good look around. I knew that crocodiles were as fast on land as in water and I didn't plan to have my leg bitten off.

I undid my bag, pulled out the leg of lamb and tied it to the thick tow rope. Then, I threw the other end of the rope over a high branch of a tree beside the water.

Then I crept to the water's edge. I dipped the bloody meat in the water and then dragged it back across the ground to my tree.

I climbed onto the branch and sat across
it. The branch rocked under my weight but
it was strong enough to hold me. I pulled on
the rope and tied it around my branch until the
lamb leg swung as bait.

Then I waited.

I waited and waited. After an hour nothing had happened and I got bored. Maybe the crocodile was feeling lazy after eating the dog.

I decided to wait another 30 minutes and if nothing happened, I would go home.

Then I heard it. The most scary sound I'd ever heard in my life.

It was a low, wild growl. My heart began to thump.

I leaned forward, trying to see the croc. I wanted to see it but I was almost too scared to look. What would it be like to see a big crocodile close up? I didn't feel safe sitting on my thin branch. Would I end up as crocodile food?

Then I saw the crocodile swimming slowly to the edge of the water.

I reached for my rucksack and my heart stopped as I saw what I'd done.

My rucksack was lying on the ground, 30 metres from the tree.

I needed my phone to take the photo –
but my phone was in the rucksack. And the
crocodile was taking my bait now.

I looked at the space between me, the bag and the beast. He had a short way to swim. I had a short way to run.

I felt sick with terror. But I had to have my phone. I had to make Toby believe me. As quick as I could, I jumped down and ran over to my bag.

The croc came at me, moving through the water like a rocket.

I screamed. I mean, really screamed.

Chapter 5

The Battle

"Run Jacob, run!" I thought as I grabbed
my bag and ran back to the tree. As soon
as I got there, I reached up and grabbed the
branch, and swung myself up.

When I looked down the beast was right below me. It was snapping its huge jaws.

You want to know what death is like? Look a crocodile in the face.

My heart thumped and my body shook as the branch bounced under me. The crocodile jumped and snapped, desperate to get at the meat.

I felt for my phone. Suddenly the rope went tight and my branch dipped down then sprang back up.

I yelled as I wobbled on the branch and nearly fell off. The rucksack fell to the ground. I pointed my camera at the beast and clicked like a madman.

The crocodile suddenly closed its huge jaws around the lamb and the rope. It pulled so hard that the tree rocked as the crocodile bit wildly at the meat.

Then the beast sprang up. It left the ground and dangled, spinning on the end of the rope, which was going down its long snout.

There was a jolt.

The crocodile's teeth had cut the rope. It crashed down with a thud. All the time I was yelling and screaming.

It moved off fast, with the lamb and tow rope in its jaws. It splashed into the water and vanished.

It was all over in a flash. But I couldn't stop shaking. I was in shock.

When I could move again, I swung down from the branch and the second I hit the ground I ran like the wind. I ran for my life.

When I got to the road I grabbed my phone and called T.T.T.

Toby listened as I told him what had happened. Then he told me to meet him in his office.

* * *

By the time I got there I was shaking from terror. I couldn't believe what had just happened.

Toby was in his office. I slammed my phone down on the desk and pushed it towards him. Then I fell into a chair and took a long breath.

"What the heck is this?" said Toby, almost laughing in my face.

He slid my phone back across to me. I snatched it up and clicked through the pictures.

Every shot was out of focus. All that I could see was a mish-mash of black, brown and green pixels. The photos were all useless.

I put my head in my hands and groaned.

What a loser.

Chapter 6

The Catch

I wasn't going to face that crocodile again,
not on my own. So I wasn't going to get any
proof. Time to give up. Gutted, I put my
phone in my bag.

Toby stood up and got me a paper cup of water. "Here," he said, handing it to me.

My hand shook as I took it from him. I drank it quickly then stood up to go.

Toby grabbed his van keys.

"You'd better show me where you took those pictures," he said.

"Oh ha, ha," I said. "I know you don't believe me. I'm going home."

"I'm not joking," said Toby. "Come on, we've got a job to do."

I got into the van and we drove to the pond. As we got closer my heart began to pound again.

"If we get out of the van, it'll kill us," I said.

Toby didn't say anything but I could see he was thinking hard.

Toby stopped the van just by the edge of the water. He turned off the engine and opened his window. We both sat watching and listening.

Then Toby got out of the van and walked up to the tree.

The end of my rope was hanging there. He held his stun stick in one hand and looked at the end of the rope. Then he bent down and looked at the ground.

What if the crocodile burst out of the water and dragged Toby into a death roll? What would I do?

Toby turned and came back.

"I suppose you're going to call me a joker," I said.

"You're no joker," he said, as he got in and slammed the door. "I'm the joker, for thinking you could get a good picture of a crocodile when it's snapping at your heels."

"So you think…" I started.

"I can see that something with big teeth has chewed that rope," said Toby. "Lots of sheep have gone missing. I thought it was a fox getting them but I bet it was the crocodile."

"And it ate a dog," I said.

"Looks like we've got a crocodile to catch," said Toby.

I punched the air. "Right on!" I said.

Chapter 7

Afterwards

I've kept the newspaper cutting of me and Toby with our crocodile in a cage. It was a big croc, over one and a half metres long.

In the end it wasn't Toby and me who caught the croc. Toby had to tell the police and then they called in the experts. But we helped.

Local boy traps croc!

The week we trapped the croc was the best week of my life.

Since then I've been working for T.T.T. every weekend. I'm going to get a job with him when I leave school.

Toby says I'm rubbish at the paper-work but I'm a great hunter. He says I saved his business and maybe someone's life.

The police think the crocodile was smuggled in when it was young, then when it got too big to handle, the owner dumped it.

We'll never know.

But if there's another croc out there, I'm ready for it.

Death Match

While the Nazis occupied Ukraine, Dynamo Kiev's footballers played matches as FC Start. Start won, again, and again. Until they faced a German army side, under the threat of death if they didn't let the occupiers win...

ISBN 978-1-4081-4263-9
RRP £5.99

Run, Jimmy, Run

Jimmy can't stand Dax's bullying any longer. He steals £150 from his father and runs away. But Dax is on the same train – and he sees the money. Now Jimmy and Dax are locked in a frantic chase. Can Jimmy run fast enough and far enough?

ISBN 978-1-4081-4259-2
RRP £5.99

The Haunted Mobile

Jake's mobile is going wrong. It's sending weird texts to his friends. Then they start to appear on his phone – from himself. A strange girl keeps calling him. He knows he has to track her down. But by the time he finds her, will it be too late for the girl – or for Jake?

ISBN 978-1-4081-4258-5
RRP £5.99